Jelly Bean Dean

May all your days be filled with
Joy & Jelly Beans :)

Tracy Stanaway

Fulton Books, Inc.
Meadville, PA

Published by Fulton Books 2020

ISBN 978-1-64952-267-2 (paperback)
ISBN 978-1-64654-336-6 (hardcover)
ISBN 978-1-64654-337-3 (digital)

Printed in the United States of America

Jelly Bean Dean

Tracy Stanaway

On April 7, a very long time ago, the most beautiful, perfect jelly bean was born. Her proud parents named her Jelly Bean Dean. Everyone exclaimed and exclaimed how beautiful she was. Such an amazing vibrant color. Look at that beautiful sparkle in her radiant blue eyes. They went on and on, and her parents agreed.

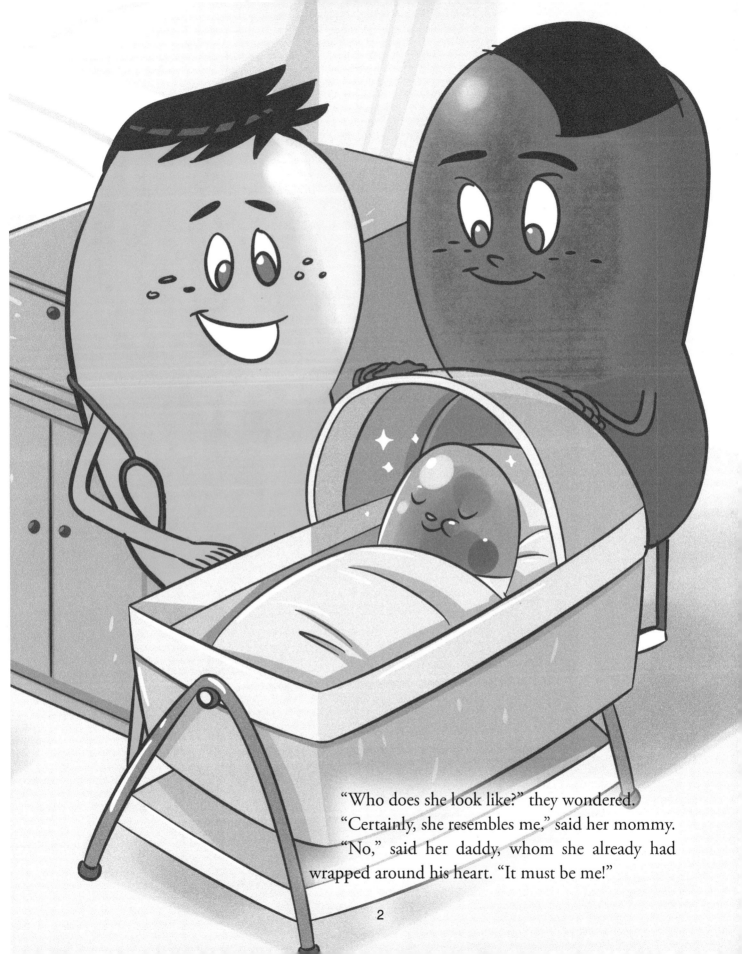

"Who does she look like?" they wondered.

"Certainly, she resembles me," said her mommy.

"No," said her daddy, whom she already had wrapped around his heart. "It must be me!"

The day finally came to take baby Jelly Bean home from the hospital. Daddy brought a teeny, tiny car seat to put her in. As Daddy was carrying out Jelly Bean though, it began to storm and poured and poured rain down from the sky. Jelly Bean's tiny blanket blew off, and she got very wet. Mommy quickly covered her up with a different blanket, and they raced to the car. Phew! All buckled in and heading home!

Back in their beautiful cottage by the sea, Mommy uncovered Jelly Bean, while Daddy was making hot chocolate for Mommy when he heard a shriek.

"Whatever is wrong, dear?" He came into the tiny family room and peered into the tiny car seat.

7

What he saw when he looked in the seat was Jelly Bean, but her gorgeous color that she had left the hospital with was gone. In place of it was a mottled, speckled Jelly Bean.

Mommy couldn't believe it. "It must have happened when she got wet from the rain. We forgot to dry her off right away!"

Daddy, always the best, just said, "She's only more beautiful now!"

Mommy though, still feeling guilty about not securing her blanket better, knowing jelly beans can't get wet unless they are dried off immediately, said, "Yes, still a lovely Jelly Bean Dean indeed!"

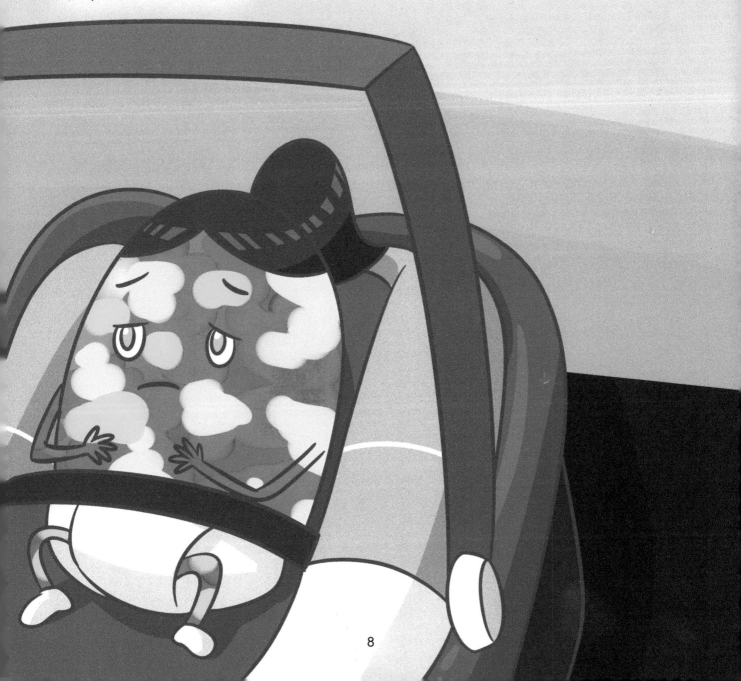

8

9

When Jelly Bean was a little older, Mommy decided to take her shopping one day. It was a beautiful sunny day, so Jelly Bean was glad she didn't have to wear a coat. As they entered the mall though, strange things began to happen. Everyone was staring at Jelly Bean and whispering.

"Look at that funny-looking jelly bean! What an awful color. Just a shame." Some other little beans even laughed.

Mommy's eyes had teardrops in them. *Why are people so cruel?* she thought. *My baby is beautiful. They just don't realize it!*

A few years went by with the same comments *everywhere* they went. When it became time for Jelly Bean's first day of school, she was fearful, but her mommy sang her this special song: "These are moments we'll remember, just you and me. I'm always here. I'll always be. When someone is cruel to you, just remember, my love—you were sprinkled with special teardrops from up above."

The big day came. Jelly Bean was up early and nervous and excited at the same time. "Today will be different, I just know it."

But it wasn't. Her classmates stared at her even more. When it came time for recess, Jelly Bean wasn't asked to do anything. She sat on the corner of the playground, trying not to cry.

Back in the classroom, her teacher, Ms. P Bean kept everyone very busy with work, so no one had time to whisper and stare, but they still did. Jelly Bean wanted to hide. She couldn't wait for school to be over.

The next day, recess was even worse. Instead of whispering, they were saying mean things even louder. She started singing her special song in a loud, clear, beautiful voice: "These are moments we'll remember, just you and me. I'm always here. I'll always be. When someone is cruel to you, just remember, my love—you were sprinkled with special teardrops from up above."

All of a sudden, she felt someone holding her hand. She looked up, and there was the most beautiful jelly bean she'd ever seen. "Hi there," a little bean said. "My name is Jelly Bean Rose. I'm sorry those other kids are mean to you, but can I be your friend? By the way, I loved your song." Jelly Bean Dean couldn't believe it! *A friend!* Yay! Yippee, *hurray!*

Ms. P's mommy always said, "There's a place for every bean, and every bean's in their right place." So the next day, Ms. P Bean sat Jelly Bean Dean and Jelly Bean Rose together in class. How wonderful that felt. Now if the others would just be nice. What Jelly Bean Dean didn't know, however, was that Jelly Bean Rose, the entire class, their parents, and Ms. P had come up with a plan.

Ms. P had been looking at the weather. She knew that it would be raining at recess. She sent Jelly Bean Dean down to the office to give Principal J Bean some papers.

As they all lined up for recess, Jelly Bean Dean saw that none of her classmates had their rain gear on and no umbrellas. She never needed hers because she knew that once a bean's color gets wet and not dried off quickly, it's too late. Jelly Bean Dean tried and tried frantically to tell all the beans to get their rain gear, but they were too excited to go out for recess.

Once outside, Jelly Bean Dean just stared in horror as, one by one, the beans started looking just like her. Ms. P very quickly called them back inside to dry off, but the strangest thing happened.

Jelly Bully Bean, the meanest bean of all, came up to her. "Look at me," he said. "Look at my cool spots right here on my arm! I look like a superhero." Another bean cried out, "And I look like a little green man from Mars!" Jelly Bean Rose thought she looked like a beautiful red robin. All the other beans were so excited to shout out what they looked like. Ms. P bean was the most beautiful of all. She looked like the most beautiful bird of paradise! The parents who had gathered with dry towels just stared at their beautiful beans in astonishment. No one even moved to dry them off. They loved their new colors.

Jelly Bean Dean, who had been watching, said in a tiny voice, "But what do I look like?"

All the beans came over to her and started saying excitedly, "Jelly Bean Dean, you look like the best of everything—the sun in the sky, sunsets at night, puppy dogs and kittens, candy bars, milkshakes, and all of our favorite things."

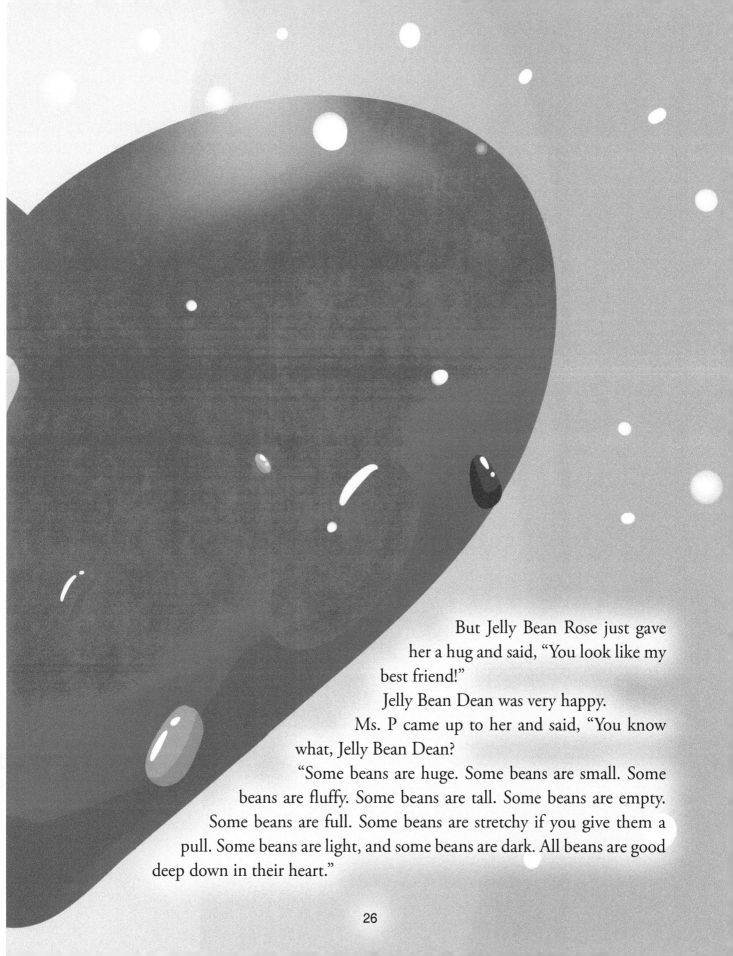

But Jelly Bean Rose just gave her a hug and said, "You look like my best friend!"

Jelly Bean Dean was very happy.

Ms. P came up to her and said, "You know what, Jelly Bean Dean?

"Some beans are huge. Some beans are small. Some beans are fluffy. Some beans are tall. Some beans are empty. Some beans are full. Some beans are stretchy if you give them a pull. Some beans are light, and some beans are dark. All beans are good deep down in their heart."

About the Author

Tracy Stanaway is a retired dance teacher and mother of three children. She lives in beautiful Montana with her husband of thirty-five years. Her hobbies include playing the piano, singing, and shopping! This book was written in memory of the original Jelly Bean Dean, Tracy's beautiful mom, Jerrine Dean. Jelly Bean Dean was her nickname all her life.